# aziz the Storyteller

To Hamid and Grant, V.H.
To Jean Pierre Makosso, S.C.

First American edition published in 2002 by
**CROCODILE BOOKS**
An imprint of Interlink Publishing Group, Inc.
99 Seventh Avenue, Brooklyn, New York 11215 and
46 Crosby Street, Northampton, Massachusetts 01060
www.interlinkbooks.com

Book design and Hand-lettering by Elisa Gutiérrez

Library of Congress Cataloging-in-Publication Data
Hughes, Vi.
   Aziz the storyteller / by Vi Hughes ; illustrated by Stefan
Czernecki.-- 1st American ed.
      p. cm.
   Summary: Although he wants to please his father and earn money
selling carpets, Aziz finds himself drawn to the storytellers in the
marketplace, including one who has a special gift meant just for him.
   ISBN 1-56656-456-5
   [1. Storytelling--Fiction. 2. Carpets--Fiction. 3. Fathers and
sons--Fiction.]   I. Czernecki, Stefan, ill. II. Title.
   PZ7.H87413 Ay 2001
   [Fic]--dc21
                                          2001006495

Printed in Hong Kong

To request our complete 48-page full-color catalog,
please call us toll free at 1-800-238-LINK, visit our
website at www.interlinkbooks.com, or write to
**Interlink Publishing**
46 Crosby Street, Northampton, MA 01060-1804
E-mail: info@interlinkbooks.com

This book was set in Adobe Sho Roman.

# Aziz the Storyteller

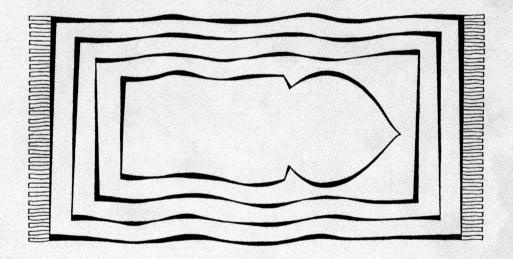

Written by Vi Hughes

Illustrated by Stefan Czernecki

Crocodile Books, USA

An imprint of Interlink Publishing Group, Inc.
New York • Northampton

Long ago, in the East, an old and weary man rose with the sun, gathered one small faded carpet, and set out for the marketplace. He journeyed through the narrow streets, finally stopping in the square.

There he waited with the carpet for the day to begin, and for a certain person to appear.

It was time.

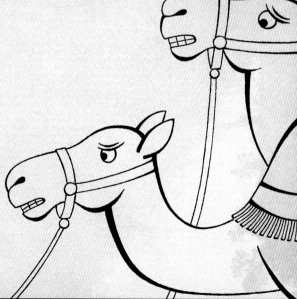

On the same day a poor rug merchant and his son, Aziz, were making their way through the narrow streets, pulling their donkey laden high with carpets. As they walked, Aziz listened to the tales of the market, collecting them and retelling them to his father. But his father scolded Aziz for wasting time with stories, when it was customers they needed.

"If you do not help me," he said, "who will provide for me when I am old?"

Anxious to please his father, Aziz went off in search of customers.

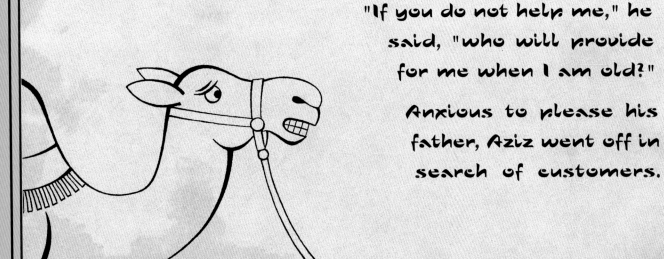

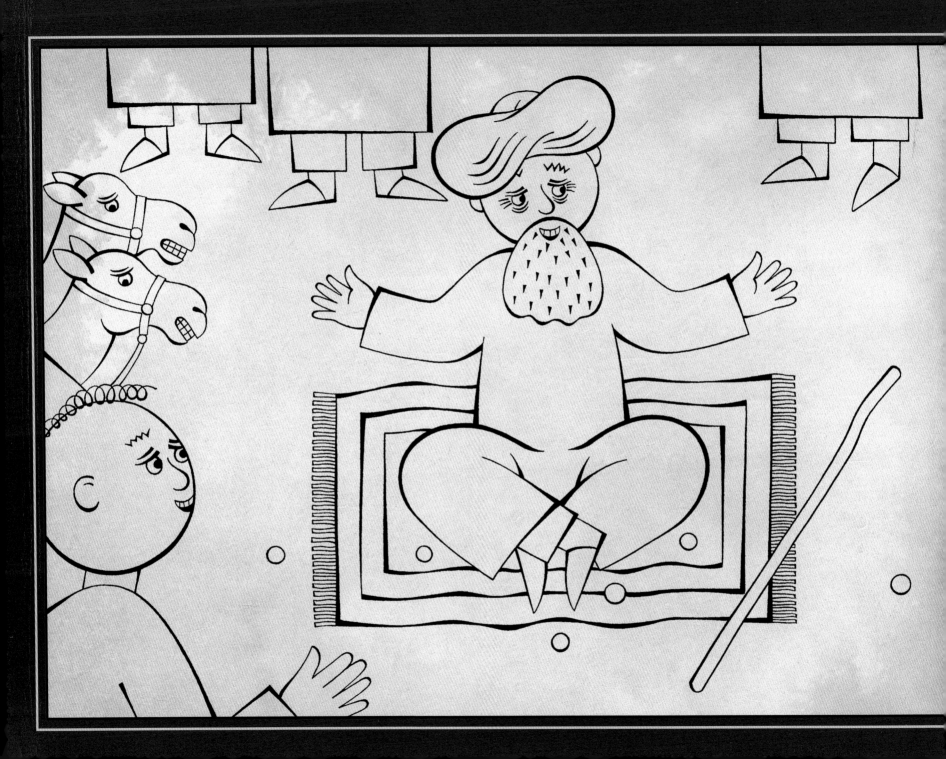

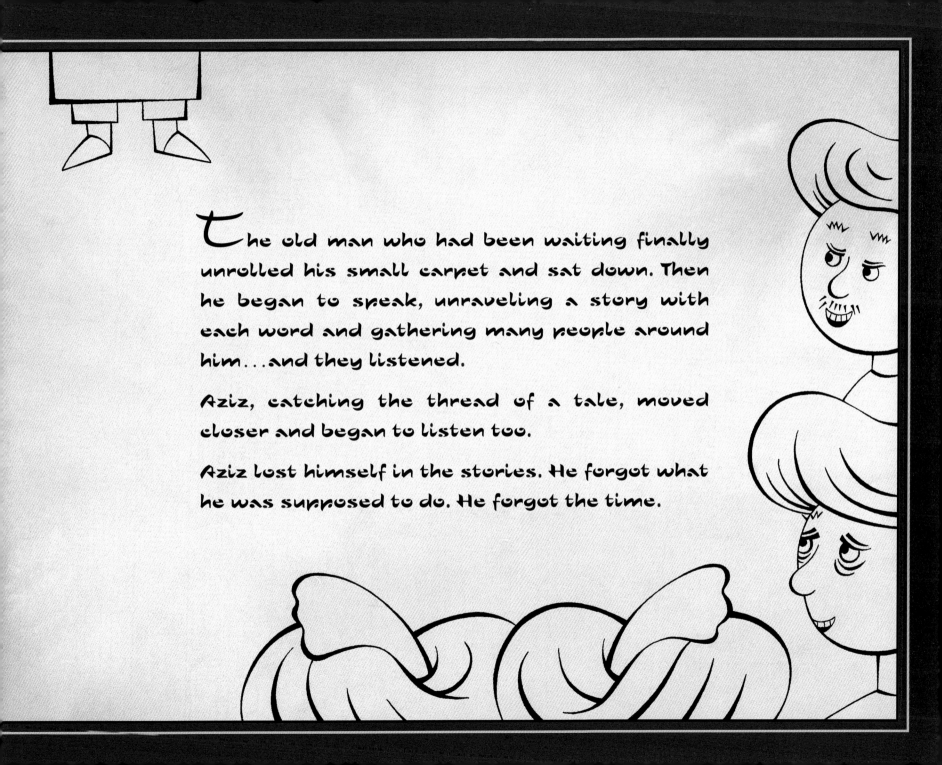

The old man who had been waiting finally unrolled his small carpet and sat down. Then he began to speak, unraveling a story with each word and gathering many people around him…and they listened.

Aziz, catching the thread of a tale, moved closer and began to listen too.

Aziz lost himself in the stories. He forgot what he was supposed to do. He forgot the time.

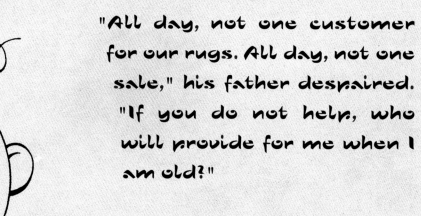

The sun was setting when he suddenly remembered his task and rushed back to his father, who asked, "Where have you been?"

Aziz could only say, "I've been listening to an old man telling stories in the square."

"All day, not one customer for our rugs. All day, not one sale," his father despaired. "If you do not help, who will provide for me when I am old?"

When the sun rose the next morning, Aziz awoke to find his father too weary to rise.

"You must take the rugs to market alone today, Aziz. Do not waste your time in idle talk."

Aziz lay the carpets in a corner of the marketplace, but he quickly forgot his father's instructions and instead listened to stories all day, capturing them, weaving them into his memory.

At sunset, worried about returning home without having sold even one carpet, he gathered the rugs and loaded his donkey. The storyteller, carrying his small carpet, approached silently.

"Will you trade your donkey for this enchanted rug?" he asked softly.

Aziz was puzzled. He looked at the old man.

"Your donkey is just what I need," continued the old man.

After a long pause, Aziz replied, "A fine donkey for an old rug? Of what use can it be?"

The old storyteller looked at Aziz closely and said, "This is a rare carpet, desired by many, but meant for you to own. It is a good bargain."

He waited. Aziz said nothing.

"This is a carpet of enchantment," the old man went on. "All the stories of the world are woven into it, tale upon tale. They will be yours to tell, for you are a storyteller too."

Still Aziz said nothing.

"By telling stories, you will provide for your father when he is old," the old man said.

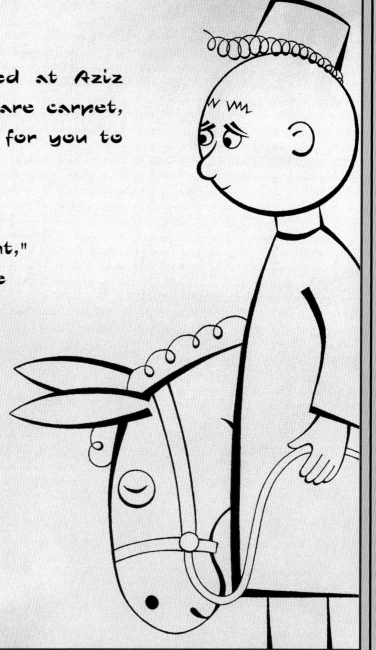

Aziz measured the man's words. How could this old storyteller know about his father? He thought and thought.... What would his father say?

But perhaps the storyteller told the truth. Perhaps the carpet truly was enchanted. He remembered how the crowd had gathered to listen.

"It is a good bargain," repeated the old man, "a carpet of stories for you to tell, a donkey to carry me, for I am old and weary."

Aziz thought some more.... Was it possible? Could he provide in this way? By telling stories?

He agreed, finally, to trade their donkey for the enchanted rug.

"Remember," said the storyteller, "carry the stories westward. When you become old and weary, pass the carpet on to another teller of tales."

*H*is father was very angry when Aziz returned home with only the rugs.

"Where is our donkey?" he shouted.

"I traded it to the storyteller for this enchanted carpet. It has all the stories of the world woven into it."

"First you waste the days gathering tales and listening to stories in the marketplace. Then you trade our donkey for nothing, only worn threads and words. Tomorrow, go back to the market. Find the storyteller. Get our donkey back!"

He despaired of such a foolish son. Who would provide for him when he was old?

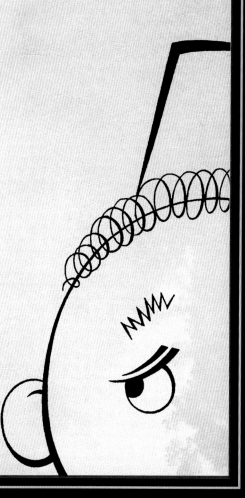

The next morning Aziz set out again, carrying the small rug. All day he searched the marketplace. He asked everyone who passed for news, but no one had seen the storyteller or their donkey. At sunset, tired and alone, Aziz unrolled the old carpet and sat down on it to rest.

The moon rose above the ancient city.

Still he sat there.

What was he to do?

He looked at the carpet beneath him.

Stories were threading their way out of the carpet, rising above into the moonlit sky, enthralling the listeners gathering in the night.... There were heroes on horseback, mystical creatures, magical beasts.

Once again Aziz lost himself in the stories.

And hundreds of coins fell.

As the moonlight faded into dawn, Aziz grew tired. He remembered his father waiting at home. His father would be worried. Aziz stood and rolled up the carpet. He gathered the coins as the crowd dispersed very quietly until only a single person remained.

It was Aziz's father, watching, his eyes shining.

"Were you listening?" Aziz asked.

"Yes."

"I can provide for you, Father, when you are old," Aziz said.

Aziz grew older and remembered the storyteller's words. He knew that he must carry the stories westward.

Leaving enough coins to last his father all his days, he set out carrying only the enchanted carpet.

Aziz traveled westward, stopping for a time in many different places.

Tales of the storyteller's magic traveled before him. Crowds gathered long before he arrived—waiting for the words, longing for adventure, seeking great truths...all the stories of the world, unraveled by the magic of the storyteller.

As the sun journeyed east to west, lighting up the sky, so did Aziz.

Many, many years later Aziz recalled the final words of the storyteller who had given him the carpet. "When you become old and weary, pass the enchanted carpet on to another teller of tales."

It was time.